Naomi's Tree

By Joy Kogawa

Illustrated by Ruth Ohi

Fitzhenry & Whiteside

First published in paperback in 2011
First published in the United States in 2009

Published in Canada by Fitzhenry & Whiteside,
195 Allstate Parkway, Markham, Ontario L3R 4T8

Published in the United States by Fitzhenry & Whiteside,
311 Washington Street, Brighton, Massachusetts 02135

www.fitzhenry.ca   godwit@fitzhenry.ca

10 9 8 7 6 5 4 3 2 1

Library and Archives Canada Cataloguing in Publication
Kogawa, Joy
Naomi's tree / Joy Kogawa ; illustrated by Ruth Ohi.
ISBN 978-1-55455-184-2
1. Japanese Canadians—Evacuation and relocation, 1942-1945—Juvenile fiction. I. Ohi, Ruth II. Title.
PS8521.O44N365 2010   jC813'.54   C2010-904391-X

U.S. Publisher Cataloging-in-Publication Data
(Library of Congress Standards)
Kogawa, Joy.
Naomi's tree / Joy Kogawa ; illustrations by Ruth Ohi.
[32] p. :   cm.
Summary: When a Japanese Canadian family is forced to leave their
home on the coast for internment during World War II, the garden's old cherry
tree sends out a song of love and peace as it patiently awaits their return.
ISBN-13: 978-1-55455-184-2 (pbk.)
1. Japanese Canadians--Evacuation and relocation, 1942-1945--Juvenile fiction.
2. Japanese Canadians – Juvenile fiction. I. Ohi, Ruth. II. Title.
[E] dc22   PZ7. K8198Naot 2010

Fitzhenry & Whiteside acknowledges with thanks the Canada Council for the Arts,
and the Ontario Arts Council for their support of our publishing program.
We acknowledge the financial support of the Government of Canada
through the Book Publishing Industry Development Program (BPIDP)
for our publishing activities.

 Canada Council
for the Arts   Conseil des Arts
du Canada   ONTARIO ARTS COUNCIL
CONSEIL DES ARTS DE L'ONTARIO

Paperback design by Kerry Designs
Original design by Wycliffe Smith Designs Inc.
Printed in Hong Kong, China

To Senator Nancy Ruth
—Joy
To those who cherish trees
—Ruth

Long ago in the Land of Morning, which is known today as Japan, a beautiful cherry tree grew. Each spring, lilting blossoms danced into view and filled the air like popcorn. And as the flowers fell in a snowy cloud, children joined hands and sang and skipped around the tree.

Soon little green cherries arrived. And one day the fruit was ripe and delicious and ready to eat.

"Ah, is this not a friendly world?" the people murmured as they feasted on the sweetness.

The Maker, who had created the world for friendship, smiled upon the cherry tree and blessed it.

So it was that, over time, the beautiful tree became known as the Friendship Tree. Mothers visited with their babies on their backs. Old people sat and rested under the peaceful branches and in the gentle, welcoming light that surrounded the tree.

And so the years went by, and the years went by. The seeds from the Friendship Tree traveled to other islands and countries far away. In the bellies of beasts, in boats, and in the beaks of many birds, they drifted and sailed and flew.

Eventually, after many years, one precious cherry seed was carried in the kimono sleeve of a young bride who sailed over the great waters to the Land Across the Sea called Canada. There, in a lovely city by the water's edge, the bride and her new husband found a pretty house with windows across the front and a big playroom in the basement.

In the backyard of the house, they planted the precious seed.

And in the spring—Ping!—up came a new baby Friendship Tree.

Over the years, the tree grew and grew, welcoming the gentle seasons of sunshine and rain.

Life inside the house grew as well. Children were born and became adults. And eventually two grandchildren, Stephen and Naomi, arrived. The children lay on blankets under the cherry tree. They watched the sparrows and robins that hopped from branch to branch. And they listened to the hushed voices of the leaves.

Naomi played with her dolls and had tea parties in the shade of the tree. And she hung upside down like a monkey from the lowest branch.

Every spring when the cherry blossoms arrived and fell in a snowy cloud, Naomi sang and skipped around the tree.

What a cheery, cherry tree you are.

What a beautiful tree you are, you are.

Later, as the season of cherries arrived, the whole family—Daddy and Mama, Stephen and Naomi—feasted on the delicious fruit.

In the evenings, Naomi looked out her bedroom window at the tree sleeping in the moonlight.

"Good night, Cherry Tree. Good night, good night," she said.

And all was well.

But the world changed. One sad day, Mama had to go far away to the Land of Morning to visit her grandmama, who was sick.

"I'll be back," Mama said as she left. Naomi waited and waited and waited. But the Land of Morning and the Land Across the Sea were now at war. Mama could not return to her family.

Great sadness filled the world. And in the Land Across the Sea, families like Naomi's, whose parents or grandparents had come from the Land of Morning, were told that they were enemies. They were all sent away from their homes, their schools, their gardens, their trees, and their friends.

The last night before she left her home, Naomi could not sleep. She tiptoed out to the backyard in the cool light of the evening. She put her arms around the tree and, looking up into the branches, said, "I wish we didn't have to leave. I wish you could talk to me, Cherry Tree. I wish we could stay with you."

The cherry tree trembled with sadness. The branches and leaves filled with soft whisperings.

Remember me, Naomi. Good-bye. Good-bye.

After the war was over, Naomi and her brother wished
with all their hearts that they could return to their house
and their happy life. But they could not. Mama had died
in the war. And strangers now lived in their old home.
All the families like Naomi's were scattered across the
country like cherry blossoms in the wind.

And so the years went by, and the years went by.
As Naomi grew older, she often dreamed about going
home. But the dream was just a dream, and it would never
come true. Finally, one day Naomi stopped thinking
about the dear house with the windows across the front.
And she stopped thinking about the cherry tree.

But the tree never stopped thinking about Naomi. The winter winds and the spring breezes carried the cherry tree's lonely song over the mountaintops to the plains.

May she be safe.

May she be kind.

May she come back again.

At night, the cherry tree's song echoed faintly in Naomi's dreams. And across the miles, the ants, the butterflies, the frogs, the worms, and other tiny creatures that leap and dart and burrow about sent their messages back to the tree.

Yes, she is safe with us.

Yes, she is kind to us.

Yes, she will come back again.

One day, many, many years later when Naomi and Stephen were old, they visited the lovely city by the water's edge. They found the street where they used to live, and they drove up and down, searching for their first home.

"Maybe it's gone," Naomi said. But just at that moment, she looked on the opposite side of the street. And there, set back behind two tall trees, stood the dear old house.

It was almost as it used to be, with the same windows across the front.

They saw that the house was empty, and out they jumped from the car.

"Should we go into the yard?" Naomi asked.

"Yes, yes," Stephen said.

They opened the gate, walked down the steps, and followed the sidewalk around to the backyard. The garage was just where it had been. Looking up, Naomi saw the windows to her bedroom, and below was the playroom door. It was all the same as before.

And then Naomi saw the cherry tree. It was an old, old tree now—scarred and bleeding with sap. But it was still alive. Someone had wrapped bandages around the wounded branches.

Naomi reached out and put her hand gently on the trunk…and suddenly she remembered everything.

She remembered lying on a blanket under the tree with her mother, listening to the whispering leaves. She remembered playing and singing and hanging like a monkey from the lowest branch. She remembered the day her mother left and the day her family was sent away from their home. And she remembered the last night when she said, "I wish you could talk to me, Cherry Tree. I wish we could stay with you."

Naomi put her arms around the tree and leaned her head on the hard, rough bark. All the tears she had not shed came flooding out.

"Dear Cherry Tree," she said softly. "My dear, dear Cherry Tree. How old we have become."

Ah, Naomi. The ragged voice of the cherry tree sighed through the leaves. *How long I have been waiting for you. How good it is to be with you again.*

And as the tree trembled so did Naomi. They were both filled with the old sadness of parting and the new happiness of meeting again. And in their trembling together, Naomi remembered Mama's last words to her— "I'll be back."

"Are you here, Mama?" Naomi whispered, putting her lips to the rough bark of the tree.

From deep, deep inside her, from a place as quiet as moonlight, she could hear her mother's voice.

Yes, my dear Naomi. You are safe with me. You are at home with me.

"Come," Naomi said, beckoning. "Listen, Stephen."

Stephen put one arm around Naomi and the other arm around the tree. He put his ear against the trunk. Softly, softly, Mama and the tree sang to them both.

May the world be safe.

May the world be kind.

May the world forever

Be our home.

"Can you hear?" Naomi asked.

Stephen nodded and smiled.

And so it was. And so it continues to be. Throughout the world, the songs of the Friendship Trees and the songs of those who love us forever fill the air like cherry blossoms in spring.

Afterword

My brother Tim and I were born in Canada, in Vancouver, B.C. When I was six years old in 1942, our family along with the entire Japanese-Canadian community on the West Coast were classified as enemy aliens and removed from our homes. All our property was confiscated. Following WWII, the community was destroyed by the government's dispersal policy, which scattered us across Canada.

On August 27, 2003, I discovered that my old family home, with the cherry tree still standing in the backyard, was for sale. On November 1, 2005, which was declared Obasan Cherry Tree Day, Councilor Jim Green and I planted a cutting from the cherry tree at Vancouver City Hall. On June 1, 2006, after a short, intense campaign, The Land Conservancy of B.C., with the help of the Save Joy Kogawa House Committee, purchased the house for a writers' center. The cherry tree, sadly, was fatally ill, but a new Friendship Tree grown from a cutting of the old tree was planted on the property. To this day, children can visit the Friendship Trees at Vancouver City Hall and at my childhood home, at 1450 West 64th Avenue.

I would like to thank with profound appreciation the work of the Save Joy Kogawa House Committee, The Land Conservancy of B.C., the writers' organizations, schoolchildren, and others too numerous to mention. Without the initial vision and heroic labor of Anton Wagner and Chris Kurata in Toronto and Ann-Marie Metten and Todd Wong in Vancouver, the house and tree would not have been saved. In particular, I wish to thank members of the Historic Joy Kogawa House Society for their ongoing commitment. Finally, I offer my deep gratitude to my dear friend, Senator Nancy Ruth, whose action made all the difference.

The original tree had white blossoms that bore fruit. This pink-blossomed tree is an artistic interpretation of that original tree.